BABAR
Visits Another Planet

Laurent de Brunhoff

BABAR

Visits Another Planet

HARRY N. ABRAMS, INC., PUBLISHERS

One beautiful day in the country of the elephants, Babar and Celeste took their children — Pom, Flora, and Alexander — on a picnic. Of course, Cousin Arthur and the little monkey, Zephir, went, too. They were all in very high spirits.

Suddenly, Arthur shouted, "Look! A rocket ship! Behind the palm trees!"

Babar laughed. "Come on, Arthur. You're dreaming." Then he said, "Oh!" in surprise. "You're right. There *is* a rocket! And it's about to land!"

The rocket landed nearby with a loud WHIRR, and the elephants were sucked inside like dust into a vacuum cleaner. Before they had time to realize what was happening, the door closed, and the rocket lifted off.

"Where is this thing taking us?" Celeste exclaimed.

Babar tried to calm her, but he was worried, too.

"There's no pilot onboard," he said. "It must be guided by remote control."

Arthur stared out the porthole, amazed, as their home, Celesteville, grew smaller and smaller. Pom, Flora, and Alexander ate cookies served by a robot, while soft, soothing noises, like music, reassured the travelers.

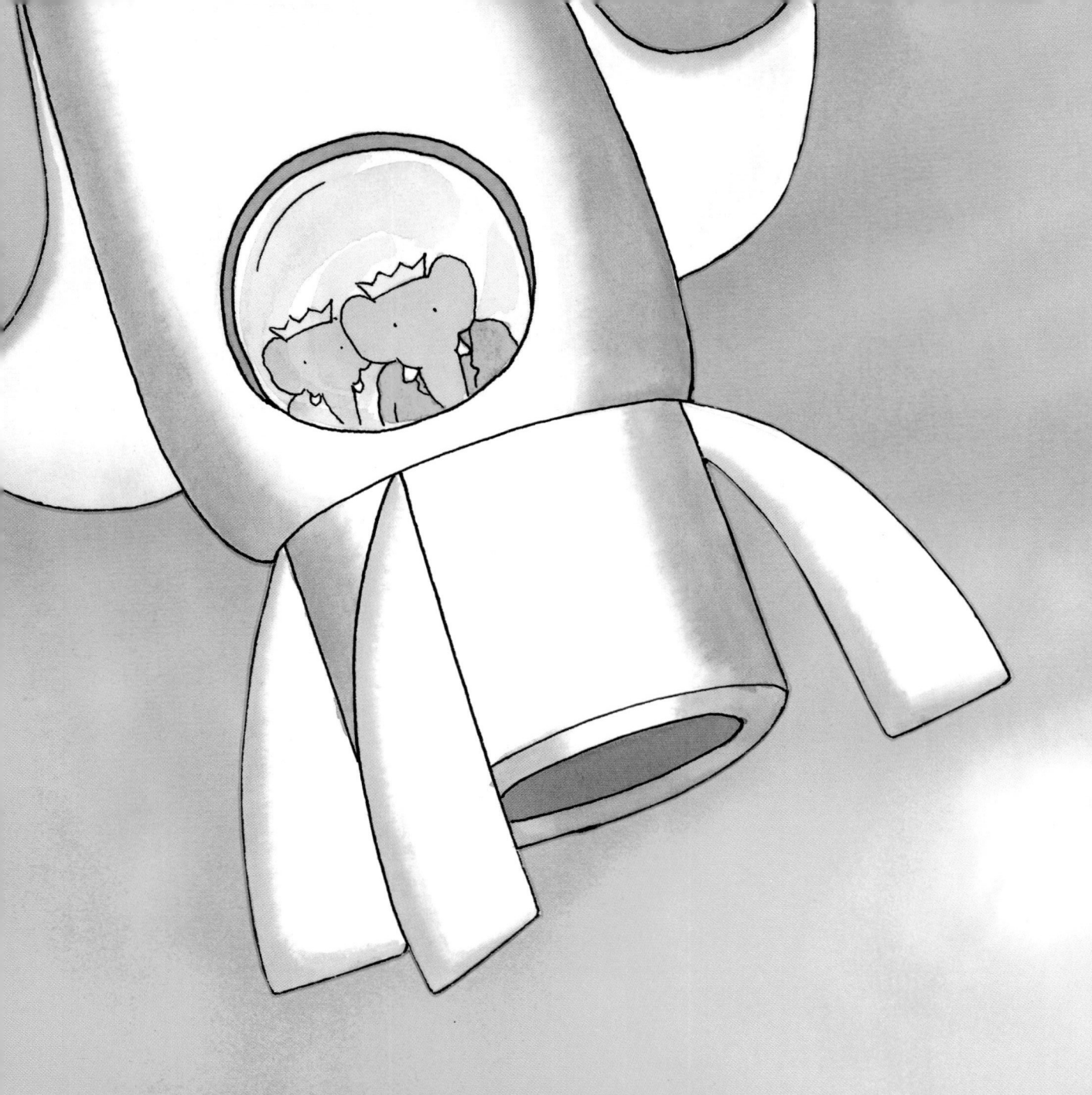

They passed the moon and the planet Mars. After many days, they neared another reddish planet. "According to my calculations," said Babar, "this planet is unknown. What will we find here?"

The rocket landed and the door opened automatically. Babar climbed down the ladder and cautiously put one foot on the ground. "Oh, dear!" he shouted. "My foot is stuck!"

Arthur burst out laughing. "Maybe this planet is made of caramel!"

Suddenly, a fleet of skimmercrafts, piloted by some strange-looking creatures, drew near the rocket. Babar, abandoning his shoe, stepped back up the ladder and said, "At least they don't look hostile." He shouted to Celeste, "Come see the inhabitants of this planet! They look like elephants, but they're not elephants."

The creatures greeted their visitors cordially in voices that sounded like clarinets.

They motioned to the elephants to join them in their skimmercrafts, and raced over the soft surface of the planet to docking platforms, where they tied up. Next, some flying eggs with seats slung underneath them floated down, and each of the curly-eared creatures grabbed one and was carried away.

"Let's do what they did," said Babar. "These flying eggs have got to be taxis."

Carrying Babar and his family, the flying eggs rose high into the air.
A city appeared, hanging from enormous red balloons. It floated,
gracefully and silently, above the mushy surface of the planet.

"This is clever," Babar observed. "How else could they live here? Houses would sink into the mud."

Celeste and the children were so astonished, they were not scared at all.

The flying eggs gently deposited the passengers on a terrace. Creatures rushed up to them. One wore a blue mushroom on his head. Another, wearing a tower of blocks, made a very long speech, "Toc, tuyip, tuyip, tic. Pituit tic tic toc."

Babar found he understood what was being said, although he did not know the language.

Mr. Tower was welcoming them to his planet. He apologized for taking them away from Celesteville with no warning. He had been perhaps too eager to make their acquaintance.

"Sir, you are right," Babar replied. "One does not pick others up in a rocket without warning. But since you meant no harm, we will not hold it against you."

Mr. Tower took them to his house, which had a swimming pool in the living room.

"Truly," said Arthur, "these curly-eared creatures know how to live." He plunged into the water and was soon joined by Pom and Alexander. Flora, in the meantime, had made a friend, a little dog with blue spots. Babar and Celeste sat chatting with Mr. Tower, learning his language.

That night they were shown to their bedrooms—little cubbies in the wall! The children climbed in quickly, but, alas, Babar and Celeste could not fit. Mr. Tower ordered the pool emptied and filled with pillows for his visitors.

"Well, this is a comfortable place," said Celeste, as she settled down to sleep, "even if it is far from home."

In the morning, Mr. Tower and Mr. Mushroom took the family out to eat. A breakfast fountain showered them with muffins and juice. It took some practice to drink neatly from such a fountain. Babar was not good at it.

Babar wanted to replace his lost shoe, so Mr. Tower took him shopping. The biggest pair of shoes in the store was not big enough, however, so Babar decided to take off his other shoe and walk in his socks.

"It will be more dignified," he said.

The next day, the creatures held a splendid tournament in the floating city. Everyone gathered in a stadium to watch the contestants try to unseat each other from the flying eggs, like knights in a jousting match.

Arthur took part. And bravo! He won! His opponent fell off his egg and into the net below. In his delight, Arthur lost his balance and he, too, fell into the net. Unlike his curly-eared opponent, he bounced like a ball.

Arthur bounced so high that he collided with his own egg-taxi, pushing it into one of the red balloons that supported the city. The balloon ripped. Arthur fell back into the net unharmed, but the spectators, scared that the grandstand might collapse, rushed off screaming.

The punctured balloon lost more and more air. The platform it held tilted dangerously.

"Quick, this way!" Babar shouted. Everyone rushed to another platform.

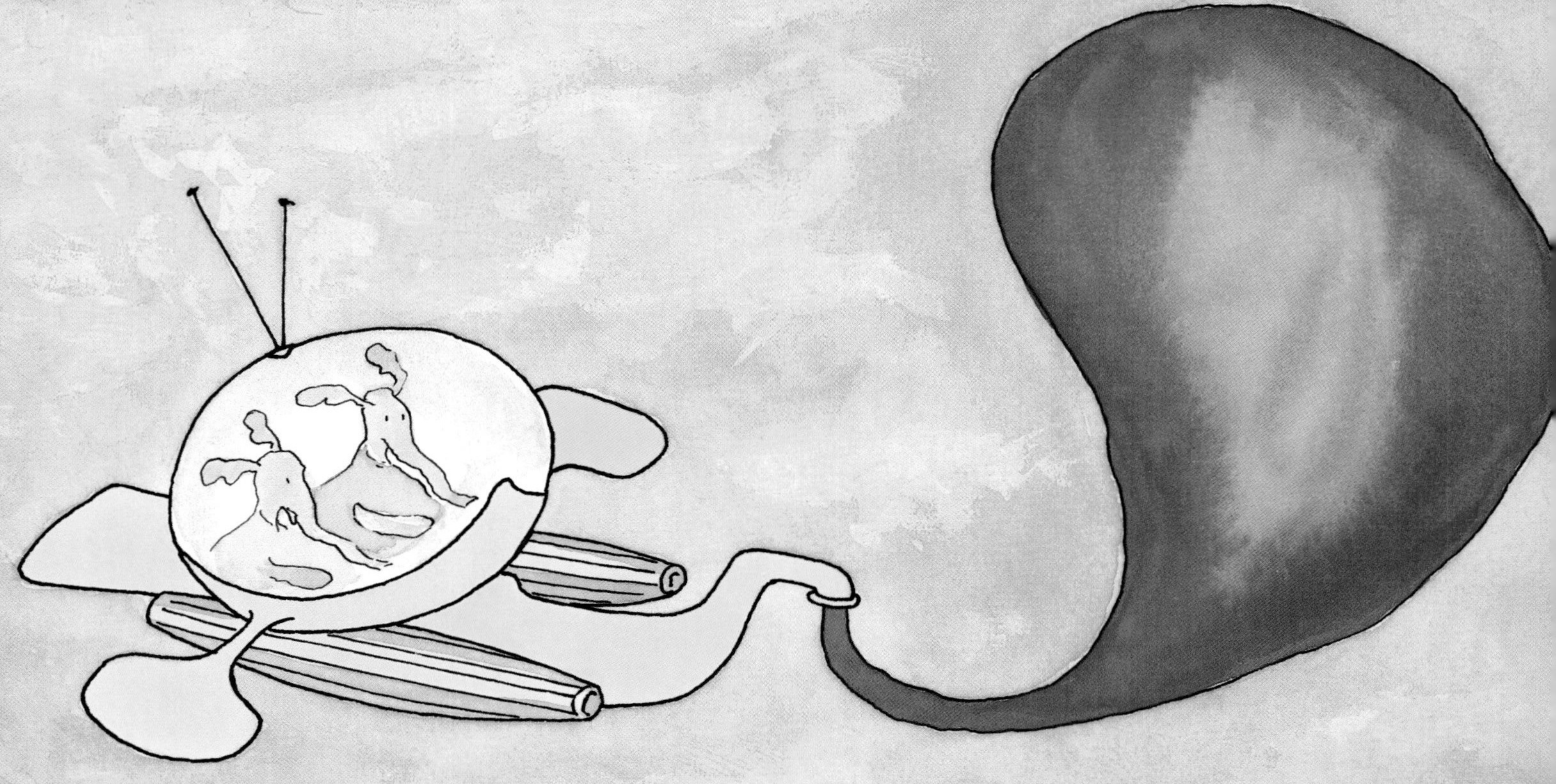

Soon a rescue crew arrived to replace the collapsed balloon. The new one was inflated as everyone watched. The platform hung securely again and the danger was over.

Babar's family rested at Mr. Tower's house. Arthur had a big lump on his head and was still dazed. Babar noticed that the creatures of the mushy planet seemed angry, and he was concerned.

"Do they think Arthur did it on purpose?" he asked Mr. Tower. (By then they understood each other well.)

Mr. Tower looked worried. He said, "I know it was an accident. But they don't. I'm sorry. I was the one who brought you all this way because I wanted to get to know you. You probably should return home now. We will say farewell. . .until another time."

"Well, next time I hope you will invite us first," said Babar, adding politely, "although we enjoyed ourselves greatly on your planet."

That night, Babar and his family left the city as they arrived, by flying egg.

Mr. Tower gave them the
adorable blue-spotted puppy
to remember their visit.
He and Mr. Mushroom and
a few others accompanied
them to their rocket and
waved good-bye as it
blasted off into space.

Back in Celesteville, they were welcomed joyfully by all their friends, who had been terribly worried about them. The little blue puppy was a great success. But their friend the Old Lady said, "It's a long way to go to get a new puppy—even one with blue spots."

"We have also brought back glorious memories of outer space and of the floating city," said Babar. "We have had a fine adventure. It isn't every day you get taken to another planet."

"I certainly hope not," said the Old Lady, giving Babar a hug.

DESIGNER, ABRAMS EDITION: DION GUTIERREZ
PRODUCTION DIRECTOR: HOPE KOTURO

The artwork for each picture is prepared using watercolor on paper.
This text is set in 16-point Comic Sans.

Library of Congress Cataloging-in-Publication Data

Brunhoff, Laurent de, 1925–
   [Babar sur la planète molle. English]
   Babar visits another planet / Laurent de Brunhoff.
     p. cm.
Summary: Babar and his family are abducted and taken by rocket ship to
an unknown planet where the residents are very hospitable and there
are many interesting sights to see.
   ISBN 0-8109-4244-5
   [1. Elephants—Fiction. 2. Extraterrestrial beings—Fiction. 3. Space
flight—Fiction.]   I. Title.
   PZ7.B82843Babif 2003
   [Fic]—dc21

2002009800